Best Wishes
Barbara Klyde
"98"

'98   Isaac Mtz

MW00981899

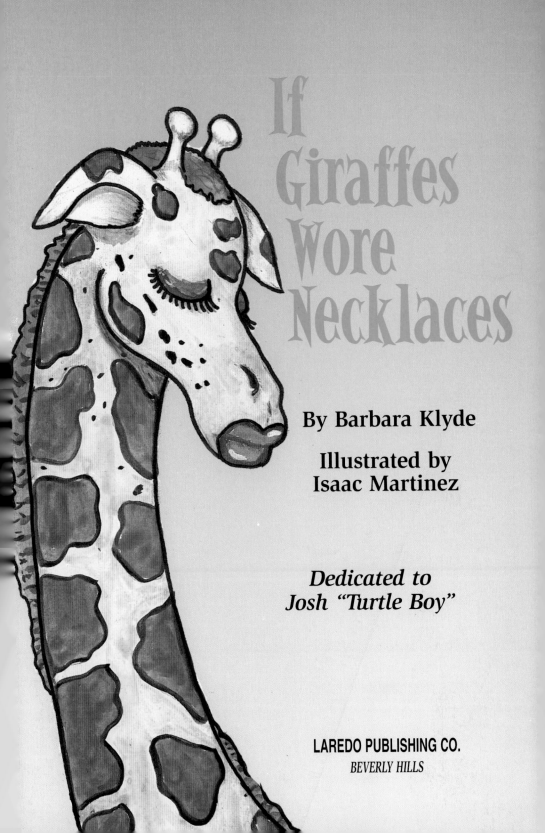

If Giraffes Wore Necklaces

By Barbara Klyde

Illustrated by
Isaac Martinez

*Dedicated to
Josh "Turtle Boy"*

LAREDO PUBLISHING CO.
BEVERLY HILLS

To John and Sandie
who helped make a dream
come true.

To Isaac
whose heart saw the story.

© copyright 1998 by Barbara Klyde
All rights reserved. No part of this book may be reproduced or transmitted in any form or by any means, electronic or mechanical, including photocopying, recording, or by any information storage and retrieval system, without permission in writing from the Publisher.

Laredo Publishing Co. Inc.
8907 Wilshire Blvd
Beverly HIlls, CA 90211
First Edition
Printed in the United States
9   8   7   6   5   4   3   2   1
Library of Congress Catalog-in Publication Data

ISBN 1-56492-251-0

If Giraffes Wore Necklaces

By Barbara Klyde

Illustrated by
Isaac Martinez

LAREDO PUBLISHING CO.
BEVERLY HILLS

If giraffes wore necklaces
how many would they wear?
I bet you think that's silly
and probably don't care.

But there was once a vain giraffe
who thought her neck was grand
She held it high for all to see
parading 'round the land.

Her nose was pointed to the sky
ignoring all below
She'd walk for days and days this way
to every place she would go.

She'd look at her reflection
for hours in the pool
Admiring her long, lean neck
this silly and vain fool.

All she'd ever do
is think about her neck
She often would forget to eat
and was a nervous wreck!

At first it didn't matter
what this giraffe would do
And it never would have mattered
if her home was in a zoo.

But her home was in a special place
with other animals and birds
To keep the peace and harmony
they'd watch their ways and words.

Now the other birds and animals
were used to giraffe's way
Pretending it didn't matter
until one eventful day.

That day it seems giraffe's habit
of walking while looking up
Caused her to stomp her foot
upon a newborn lion pup!

The lion's mom was angry
at what giraffe had done
She called her friends together
while comforting her son.

The animals and birds all came,
the moon was large and bright
Whispering for hours and hours
on this important night.

The next day they all waited
until giraffe walked by
And so she did as usual
her nose up to the sky.

"Hello, Giraffe," called gopher
Of course she didn't hear
"Hello!" again he hollered
but it never reached her ear.

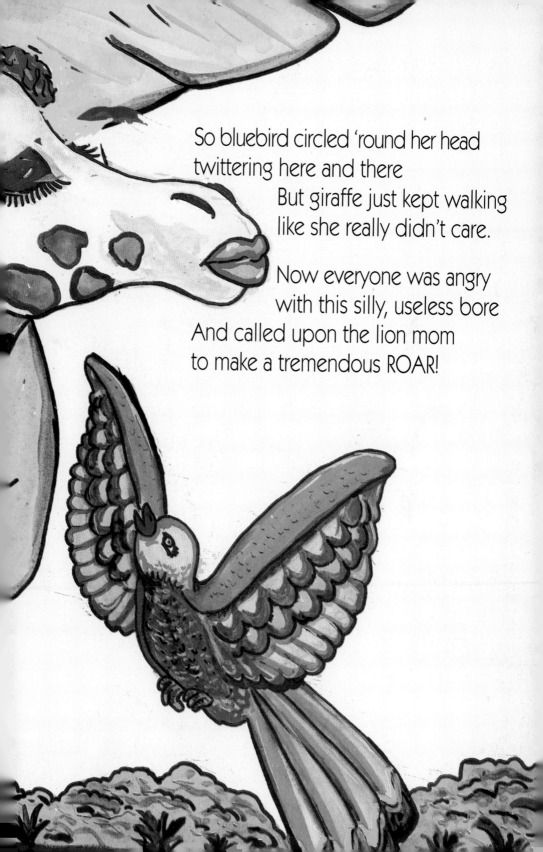

So bluebird circled 'round her head
twittering here and there
But giraffe just kept walking
like she really didn't care.

Now everyone was angry
with this silly, useless bore
And called upon the lion mom
to make a tremendous ROAR!

The giraffe then stopped walking
flustered by the noise
Trying to look dignified
regaining all her poise.

"Yes?" she quietly replied
"Is there something I can do?
Is there something I can get
like a tasty leaf or two?"

Gathering his courage
the gopher now spoke loud
"Oh no, giraffe," he shouted
applauded by the crowd.

"We want to give you something
because your neck is grand
And you can wear it every day
parading 'round the land."

Giraffe was surprised and pleased
to see the gift below
A lovely golden necklace
ablaze with sunshine glow.

"Please bend your neck" asked gopher
in a very pleasant voice
"So I may place this necklace
on the only proper choice."

The giraffe quickly lowered
her body toward the ground
And gopher put the necklace on
while the others gathered round.

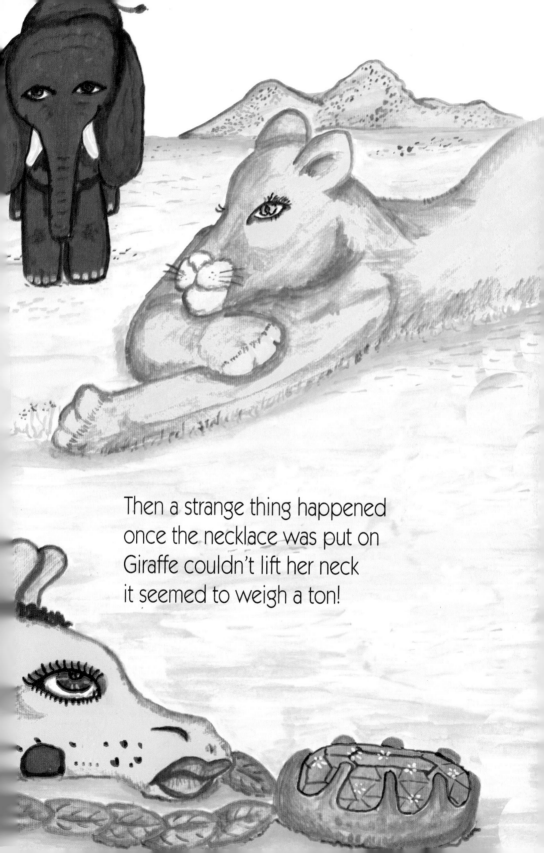

Then a strange thing happened
once the necklace was put on
Giraffe couldn't lift her neck
it seemed to weigh a ton!

The animals began to laugh
at the funny sight to see
Giraffe's neck stuck on the ground
with a necklace too heavy!

Tears were filling giraffe's eyes
she knew what she had done
Her vanity had caused her pain
The others, they had won!

"We're sorry to have fooled you"
the gopher said out loud
"We're sorry that we fooled you"
repeated all the crowd.

"Please, just remove the necklace
I will never again be
That vain and stupid giraffe
her head up in a tree."

"I promise I will be aware
of everybody's needs
And spend more of my time
practicing good deeds."

Together the animals and birds
took the necklace from her neck
And hung it up for all to see
lest anyone forget!

About the Author

Barbara Klyde grew up in Buffalo, New York, and after graduating from the University of Buffalo, continued her education at Wichita State University Physician Assistant Program where she completed her training in Family Medicine and Post Graduate Residency in Emergency Medicine in Northern California. She has been practicing for the past twenty years.
She has been writing ever since she can remember, and has two poems published with the National Society of Poets. She is a member of the Society of Children's Writers and Illustrators, and is pleased to present her first children's book,
"If Giraffes Wore Necklaces."
Barbara lives in Southern California, where her two sons also reside.

About the Illustrator

Isaac Martinez is a self-taught artist who loves to draw, play volleyball on the beach and take long walks on the sand. Meditation and being creative are part of his hobbies. He wants "If Giraffes Wore Necklaces" to carry message of unity and love as well as a lesson in caring and respect for the environment. His fresh talent and whimsical illustrations awaken the creativity in children. Isaac lives in Long Beach California. This is his first book.